"Six insidious stories. ... mprise Ira Rat's ... uirming for mo ... FIXION, "(A)nxi ...

... Hands, and The Couvade)

"Rat somehow captures a fistful of psychic fragments from the ether and tosses them right into your open eyes. Every story is saturated in a recognisable contemporary angst and apathy - yet the prose is still propulsive, as if Rat's sheer dynamism of craft is enough to animate even the most jaded post-covid consciousness into a powerful metaphor."

– **Chris Kelso** (author, *The Dregs Trilogy*)

" Ira Rat peels layers of spectacle away from the perception we would like to have to reveal the insidiously grotesque reality beneath. Everything he writes feels like he has something to show us or to make us understand, if only for the small comfort of sharing tragedies."

– **Charlene Elsby** (author, *The Devil Thinks I'm Pretty* and *Violent Faculties*)

FOR EMILY

"HAIRS"

Copyright © 2023/2024 Ira Rat
Book & cover design by Ira Rat

This is a work of fiction. Names, characters, businesses, places, events, locales, and incidents are either the products of the author's imagination or used in a fictitious manner. Any resemblance to actual persons, living or dead, or actual events is purely coincidental.

This book may not be reproduced in whole or in part, except for the inclusion of brief quotations in a review, without permission in writing from the author or publisher. No part of this publication may be reproduced, stored in or introduced into retrieval system, or transmitted, in any form, or by any means (electronic, mechanical, photocopying, recording, or otherwise), without prior permission of the publisher.

Requests for permission should be directed to
filthylootpress@gmail.com

SECOND "DELUXE" EDITION

"HAIRS"
BY IRA RAT

Filthy Loot

filthyloot.com

Thanks to Sadie Hartman, Joe Koch,
Chris Kelso, Charlene Elsby,
Rebecca Rowland, Sam Richard,
Cody Goodfellow, Jon Steffens, and others.

And a special thanks to Dennis Cooper for including
the first edition of this book in
his 2023 year-end list.

Introduction

I often have writers, editors, and readers tell me that I should continue a story past where its natural for me to cut and run.

This feels like lingering too long while peeping through an open window. Selfishly, I don't want to get caught – and for that, I'm sorry.

-Ira. June, 2023

At the Base of a Crucifixion

You are the same decaying meat as everything else, the mirror read in the jagged runes of a seasoned street tagger. Honestly, I thought, I've seen much worse hanging in dozens of holier-than-thou galleries throughout the Midwest. The pockmarked mirror was chipped from the other side, warping its reflection of the reality it was manufactured to portray. The message is a little too *Fight Club*, the aesthetic a little too on-the-nose-Juxtapoz-my-book-is-available-at-Printed-Matter wannabe, but I'm sure I could have made a couple of grand off it if it had come into my gallery.

Ah, to be young again and freely dispensing mid-level art to anybody just wanting to take a shit.

Water dripped from my face into the basin. My hangover clinging to my skin like a latex mask I couldn't scrub away. I open my mouth and look for the lingering source of the rancid Tic-Tac and cigarette taste. I'm not sure what I'm looking for, but I'll know it when I see it.

Occupied! I chide to the persistent jingle of the handle. It's the third time in as many minutes. I stop and take pleasure in the thought that someone on the other side is standing there with their guts churning. The best thing to have is what somebody else wants, even if it's just this coveted side of the bathroom door.

My eyes are red, but I vaguely remember that they've been that way for years. Professional hazard; I make my living from seeing things. I reach over, flush the toilet, and stand there scrolling through High Snobbery, screen-capturing a Yayoi Kusama-inspired cardigan that costs more than most of these artists' yearly rent.

Let the Philistine wait.

The thought that anybody acted as coolly sophisticated as they do on this side of the double-paned glass doors with the gallery's name (always in Helvetica Bold) when that glass was keeping out the smell of cow shit, pig shit, the smell of people in John Deere hats, and believe me, they do have a distinctive smell — was amusing in a way that I can't quite place.

Have I been here before? Deja vu sneaks up whenever I enter a gallery. The same influences. The same pieces. It would be sad if it weren't all so familiar. On this side of the Swedish-inspired signage, it's always the same quietly creaky neutral wood floors, white walls, and man-buns explaining to their bored and teased girlfriends what a piece means. I always mused that it must be the tax that pretty blond girls pay to piss off their parents.

The slow hum of a single tone played ad infinitum vibrates the air in a way that neither inspires curiosity nor drowns out the endless drivel spewing from man-bun's triple-pierced lip.

Here's where someone once saw a Cy Twombly and decided they could drop out of art school. Here's the Kiki Smith clone. Here's the (my bowels rumble) Warhol of mediocrity. By the child-like scrawl of "corn" that had been scribbled out, this one thinks they're the Basquiat of the Midwest. They all should have stayed in the system, graduated, and become professors, passing on the lineage of mediocrity that is the bread and butter of the industry.

I stop momentarily at a beautifully rendered portrait of a woman in charcoal. It exudes a skill that would take decades of intense training to do. It's also dull as fuck, and nobody would look at it twice, even if it where the cover of New American Painting.

I make my living selling boring to the bored. Beyond a few household names, anything new or interesting is promptly forgotten because it didn't go well over the couch. Destined to die in obscurity, but isn't everything? It's the burden of the bourgeoisie and haute culture that is medicated to the gills when anxiety is still the highest form of art.

I spot someone standing in the corner. Completely nude. Shivering. Their untamed body hair covers any overt signs of their gender. Their slight weight flattens out their chest and hollows their empty belly. Their head is shaved. Even nude, they exude indigent chic. Eyes closed, sensual lips drawn into a neutral expression. Just waiting to be recognized and bought.

They hold an antique razor in one effete hand, slowly dragging the edge along the other. They peel the skin from the tip of their middle finger to their wrist in a perverse mimicry of pulling on a surgeon's glove. Even with the slight wet snap, I do not see their face waver from its cold, calculated distance.

Interesting, but there's no money to be made in performance. Unless you're Matthew Barney or Abramović, *they* even had to figure out how to sell a few trinkets.

Deliberately, their dewy eyes open as if seeing the world for the first time, and in the faux-baritone voice of a child trying to sound much older ask: "Are you done in there?"

Cute. I began fumbling in my pocket for a loose pill to swallow dry. The screen of my phone immediately lights up when I look at it. I see that my Uber is ready to take me somewhere else and then somewhere else.

Ad nauseum, amen.

A Hair

Looking in the mirror, I found a single, thick black hair growing out of my cheek. I found its placement and ruggedness odd, the kind of hair growing out of a witch's wart. I had to pull at it with my fingers to find that it was, in fact, a part of me.

The rest of my face was electrolysis smooth — a significant investment from a rather anemic inheritance. I had been pleased with said investment until now.

Aging is just a mild embarrassment created for societal control. I think someone said that. But I say: Only the poor get old. It's my mantra. My bathroom was white, sparkling white, the kind of white that screamed "wealth," "luxury," and "youth," but none of those qualities were in steady decline.

Jesus wept.

I bent down to pull tweezers out of a drawer, but

it was gone when I looked at myself again. Anxiety crept into my bones. I searched and couldn't find it. It was so thick and monstrous that there was no way it could hide in my fluorescent haven.

There were rows and rows of dingy orange bottles, but for the life of me, I didn't know what a single one of them did. Nor did I care as long as they did their job.

In this case, they kept me alive and hid the pain behind a stone wall. That's all I asked for.

The pale vanity light created a pink mist behind my eyelids. Its heat warmed my face. I remember hearing that these long light tubes contain chemicals that cause cancer. Their light can burn your skin.

I haven't seen any evidence of this, but I dim them out of reflex. *Too careful is never too careful,* as Mother used to say. My sigh rings, "I wish I had a cigarette." My tapping foot mimics my heart pounding out of my chest.

I reach into my bathrobe to find my phone. I'm a cliché, but I'm trying hard not to be. These devices are morally bankrupt, but I always have one on me. I dim the screen, remembering what I read about blue light.

Cancer causes cancer-causing cancers. You've got to avoid them at all costs. My first memory of my mother is her holding her fingers like a bunny, quoting. *I'm late! I'm late!*

The last is crying over a radiated husk.

On my hands and knees, I use the flashlight to search for the hair. It must be here somewhere. I inspect every nook and cranny but fear I'll never find it.

Jesus Loves Me

"Jesus loves me, this I—" A burst of scalding hot water on her wrists stunned Amy silent.

Amy gagged from the overly bleached smell of the bathroom, the harsh odor mingling with the pool water smell of the hot tap water, an antiseptic cocktail that kept her breathing short.

"No!" her mother cried out dispassionately before bursting into a coughing fit. "Again!" She blocked the drain with a white rubber stopper, letting the water fill the basin. "What would the Son of God think if He heard this atrocity?" she asked through the blue smoke rising from the cigarette dangling from her lip. She crossed herself. "I said *sing it*!"

"Jesus lo—"

Amy felt the full force of her mother's hand as she grabbed her neck and submerged her face in hot water. Even through the water, she could hear her mother's wheezing.

Amy's legs nearly gave out, her feet failing to find a grip on the stool she stood on before the white porcelain altar of the bathroom sink, like the pleading feet of a man about to be hung.

Though her face glowed a bright tomato-red, it had never been scalded so bad as not to fade back to a rosy peach in an hour or so.

"Again." Her mother demanded from within another spasm of coughs. A bottle of bleach was in her hand, and she slowly began adding it to the water.

"Jesus loves me, this I know, for the Bible tells me—"

Her mother plunged her face into the sink.

"Not good enough! What will Father Mayhew think if you don't sing it like a little eff-ing angel?" More coughs, always more.

Amy didn't want to know what Father Mayhew would do to her; she'd heard things.

Deep down, Amy knew that none of this was uncalled for. She knew her mother was trying to raise her to be the best little girl she could be. She knew it because that's what Mom always said.

Through the fog of the glass, she saw the little blue dot just above the collar on her mother's chest, the tattoo that showed the doctors exactly where to aim their treatments.

A slow boil erupted in her tummy. Worried that something would happen to her mommy before she was done helping her become the best.

Otherwise, how would she ever get to heaven?

That Constant Irritation

(originally appeared in *Dirt in the Sky*)

> "It was really wild
> She started out nude & put
> on her clothes"
>
> - Jim Morrison (Paris Journal)

Amy's on her shit again. This constant, irritating whine comes from the air raid siren in her mouth. Fortunately for me, though, I had already tuned out before she even started in on all of it. If history is anything, and it always is, it's the same bullshit she's been on for the last couple of weeks. Something about that actor, Armie Hammer, and how the father on some children's show had done things to her that would make that millionaire heir to a baking powder empire look like Father Teresa.

Amy showed Erica the teeth marks on the small of her back. When he drove back to his wife's place in the Reseda, it looked like he had taken more than a mouth full of her cheap porcelain-colored skin with him. Hollywood isn't a meat market but markets meat better than anywhere else. In this town, even our vegans are cannibalistic.

Hand to God, I don't know which one is worse, going around looking like a used piece of Dubble Bubble or admitting that you had been fucking around with someone on basic cable. Amy was doing both on full display to anybody who walked by the booth's retro green sparkle faux leather. I wouldn't be surprised if she hadn't already added it to her resume.

Bold headline: Special Skills. The following line, Languages: Spanish (Passing). Next Line, Improv (2 classes). The following line, getting barebacked by basic cable stars and driving them into cannibalistic rages as they deposit their seed into my orifices (versatile).

A line of K goes up her nose and is quickly followed by its brother. The wrapper of a Pixie Stick being used in lieu of a straw. She briefly stares at the last one like a 600-lbs-lifer looking at the last Twinkie in the box. The restraint she shows must be self-glorifying. She's already slurring her words and looking like she's about to fall asleep, but she's here, the line is here, and the temptation of ditching her self-restraint creates a static in the air.

She snorts it and does a pitch-perfect Uma Thurman. "I said *Goddamn*." It's hard to beat a classic. When everything is a reference to something in the over-culture, finding the one that fits your personality can be tough. This one doesn't suit her. Amy's dishwater blond hair is scraggly, and her thrifted clothes look more Depop than vintage. She looks like she should be in line to go into a Starbucks rather than the Viper Room. I do a quick "Our River" prayer before blowing a kiss to the ceiling.

The first rule of Hollywood is to be a cliché. There are other rules.

The way she keeps going on and on, you'd think that she was doing coke in the middle of this faux-fifties monstrosity of a restaurant, but no. I had to be friends with the only person on earth who got talkative on anesthetics, but I digress.

If I had a dollar for every time, I heard some

young neverwillbe cry "woe-is-me," I wouldn't need to be meeting my father for lunch in half an hour. Erase that. I probably still would. Trading idle time for free food and enough money to subsist for a family of four, for a month is hard to play off. But at least the extra money would keep me from dealing with Z-listers and their complaints.

I realize this is a catch-22 situation, but let's just fix that in post. There's no reason to get lost in the weeds when I'm telling you about these people. They're nothing, but then again, to the world at large, so am I. I don't even have an Instagram. We are all just background fodder in the cattle call of life.

Amy is an aspiring teen star that is too visibly aged to pass as anything younger than 30. However, she is sixteen and isn't even convincing as herself. Erica is a wouldbe pop star that couldn't hit a note if she were Princess Di, and the note was a pilon. The fact that she looked practically geriatric wasn't going to land her on American Idol.

Nobody is the doe-eyed, perfect-haired,

perpetually youthful former Disney star that you see on the front cover of magazines. They grow those in a lab somewhere outside of Orange County.

I probably wouldn't have even mentioned Erica if she hadn't been the living furniture to which Amy was showing off her bites *this time*. It could have been anybody else, literally anyone, but in this case, it was Erica. In the tell-all I write, it'll be a dewy nymphet semi-celebrity that I won't name for the sake of her career.

The streets of Hollywood are awash with homeless people's shit and zeros like us. Toned, well-dressed, and vacuous. A dime a dozen would be overvaluing us by at least nine cents. Well, when I say that, I mean—they are. I, your humble narrator here, well... I'm fabulous. I love me. If the goddess Kondo was to hold me, she would tell the world that I sparked joy.

I repeat these aphorisms to myself so I don't go spiraling. Side effects of the K. I don't want to dissociate completely. Just be dissociative enough to be marvelous. Like one of those kids from Euphoria, but with fundamentally marketable skills other than knowing what producer's cock to suck or where to score.

I know those things too, but I haven't bothered to utilize that knowledge *yet*. If there was one thing that I didn't want to subject myself to, it would become big enough to become tabloid fodder. Jesus wept as the altar boy fiddled under his loincloth— our Zendaya who art in Beverly, hollow be thy name.

As a rule, everybody in Hollywood has to act like they don't want to be famous. There are others…

Something inside me starts eating away at my stomach. It's probably time to go to lunch. Either that or it was just the general-everyday-type anxiety that I've become accustomed to since I got emancipated three years ago, moving from a McMansion in the Hills to a $1,000-a-month loft downtown. I say loft, but it's, in all reality, a closet. My neighbors are cam girls and junkies, but that's beside the point. Deep down, aren't we all cam girls and junkies?

HAIRS

My father is a producer, but I'm unsure what he's produced. I've been meaning to look at his IMDb page. But it's something that's slipped my mind for the past decade or so. In all actuality, I'm worried that I'd go there, and he was one of the people who unleashed the Kardashians into the world. His Venmos always make their way into my account, and that's all that really matters. He could be producing Kirk Cameron movies for all I care.

The faintest drop of blood sits in the corner of his mouth as he drinks his lunch, three fingers of Blue on the rocks. We all have our vices. Mine is ordering the most expensive thing on the menu and then not giving him the satisfaction of eating it in front of him.

He made a dramatic gesture of transferring over the fare for the Lyft over, his gadget sparkling and new, fresh from the Genius Bar. I look at the cracked screen of my Galaxy III and see that it had been sent with a note. *Love, Daddy*. It makes my bowels quiver, but I try not to let it get to me. He only shows this kind of loving-father BS when he wants something.

I see him pouring something into his drink from a small vial.

He sent me flowers when he asked me to move out. Before I was even old enough to drive, mind you. Fuck, I'm still not. The legality of my emancipation notwithstanding, he was an asshole of the highest caliber, but so much so that you had to *respect* the balls that he had his assistant cradle while she earned her salary.

Don't even get me started on the dirt that I've got on this literal motherfucker. When I finally get around to writing *Daddy Dearest*—which, I'm sure, will be the most massive of hits and will be turned into a movie, it will probably star Bradley Cooper or some other aging actor who'll be 100 times better-looking, charming, and realistic than the man in front of me.

He smiles a big toothy off-red grin. He looks like a vampire in some b-movie that would air late at night on one of the local stations.

Something inside me starts eating away at my stomach again, but giving this prick the satisfaction of seeing me eat would be too much for me to stand. However, exhibiting signs of anorexia in front of the man who put me on a diet when I was three might be its own sick gratification.

Two rules of LA, you can never be too thin or too much of an asshole to absolutely everyone around you. There are other rules…

"So, how have you been?" he asks with the smug charm of a frat boy who just got caught in his first panty raid.

I say nothing in response. I just stare out the window looking at the low-rent glamorati parading outside the restaurant like it's fashion week. The lousy dye jobs and Shein-level fast fashion bullshit knockoff clothing is nearly intolerable, but at least I wasn't related to them.

"Well, Daddy, I'm just so appreciative of all the things that you do for me every day. Busting your ass to ensure I live in the lap of luxury in the greatest city on the planet."

He paused to wallow in his own amusement.

"Why thank you, *offspring*. It's the least I could do."

Even though I had done enough animal tranquilizers to subdue Noah's ark, I use all my effort to unclench my fist. I try to relax my jaw, but I hear the nails on a chalkboard sound of my teeth grinding.

Another rule of Hollywood is to rely on test marketing. Don't forget to fill out your survey before getting your payout.

Here's a snippet from my unwritten book about my father.

Shortly before he showed me the door, I would walk home from school in eighth grade. Most kids would, but it's a 4-mile round trip between my home and school. As I had said before, I had been a chubby kid, so it had been his idea.

No matter the weather, I made the death march to and from St. Albert's every day. On this day, though, it had been scorching, the kind of heat where you would see science teachers demonstrating the cooking power of the sidewalks. I was sweating like a pig. The sweat under my belly fat was sizzling like bacon. I felt like Wile E. Coyote in one of those scenes where he's crawling through the desert.

Anyway, before I get too hung up on that. On this particular day, I walked into the kitchen door, and there was my father, pants around his ankles, jerking off. In the final version, I'll get all purple prose about the veins standing out on his forehead and the off-tan color of his cock. With the shock of seeing exactly where you came from, the crowd nervously chuckles, but do you want to know the kicker? Sitting there, open, on the kitchen table was my yearbook. My fucking *seventh-grade* yearbook. I'd made a bigger deal out of it at the time, but being a producer in Hollywood who was into jailbait was beyond cliché.

Who out there is willing to give me a book deal?

A Muzak version of "L.A. Woman" plays at a whisper as the silence between us grows.

An Iowa Story

It had crossed my mind how easy it would be to snap this cocksucker's neck right here. I doubt that anybody would miss him. Hope's a small town, but from the look of his highly polished gray boots, he probably came from Cedar Rapids or Des Moines. Even then, someone would probably end up reporting the missing prick.

Though, once I had this limp-dick's neck turned the wrong way round. All I would have to do is roll him over the rail of the pen. Sure, the wood is so rotten that it might snap, but it wouldn't be that hard to do, and the hogs would take care of the rest.

They have hungry eyes, and he looks like he's well-fed. Better fed than they have been the last couple of years. His lady-like fingers were as fat as sausages.

Of course, they're too chickenshit to send somebody from town to tell me that you have 30 days to get off the land, my family has lived and worked for the past three generations. Hell, they probably knew that I wouldn't have even answered the door if it was that *other* fuckin' piece of shit from the bank, Calvin.

I already told *that* pinstriped asshole what I would do to him the next time I saw him. Watching his nose gush red and sticky all over his tie as the armed guards pulled me off him, a pretty little picture in my mind.

The pigs were too old to breed, too haggard to slaughter. Lately, I'd had been letting them live out their remaining time in dead-eyed peace as they roamed the pen, though now I didn't have enough money to keep them fed properly. The only time they got a meal was when one of the others kicked it, kind of like a piggy version of a Donner Party.

At least they knew how to care for themselves, unlike those so-called factory pigs that can't even step outside without catching their death.

This prissy little fuck would be nothing but bones in seconds. From the look of it — they're already sizing him up. Bones aren't hard to get rid of. They never are.

I pictured taking my knife, cutting through his sinew, and separating his bones before throwing them in the chipper.

Doing it might not solve all my problems. The bank would send the next jackass in a week or so to serve me with more papers. Telling me that my Great-grandfather's farm was not theirs'. Though no doubt, both me and the pigs would get a certain amount of satisfaction as I watched his soft, manicured hands being fought over like the last piece of fried chicken at Sunday dinner.

"Mr. Olsson," he said out the side of his smug little face, "it doesn't give me pleasure to be the bearer of bad news," I told him that I knew and understood. He droned on and on, but all I heard were the pigs as they rooted in the mud and oinked to each other.

Finally, he reached out his hand, and I reluctantly shook it, trying to break the bird-like bones.

HAIRS

I pictured grabbing his tie and shoving his face between the posts. Watching his smug little smile get pulled off his skull by the hungry animals within. What would that get me? Another month?

A month ain't shit.

As quickly as he came in, he strolled off to his pussy little toy car and was gone. Any thoughts of what I wanted to do to him are now the daydreams of an old kook, one screw turn away from the loony bin.

Alone, I watched the pigs stick their hungry snouts out into the world. If I had any balls at all, I would have just knocked the fence down and let them fend for themselves.

Instead, I unlatched the gate and closed it behind me. I pet Abbie. She's as big as a truck but so underfed that you could see its ribs. Albino, pale and nearly blind, Abbie grunts approvingly. Her tongue licked the edge of my knife. She began nudging my hand as I lay down.

I'm the Last Person I'd Want to Be

(originally appeared in *Stories of the Eye*)

> "(T)here are things we can't see now, that are there, that are embedded, that it takes time in order to be able to see."
>
> - Lynn Hershman Leeson

When I was 7, my father hit me so hard in the chest that I felt my soul leave my body.

Stop doing that, he said.

I still don't know what I had been doing, but I was damn sure never to do anything again.

1973

"Jesus, what a shithole." The apartment is one

coat of fresh paint above a skid row flophouse: open kitchen, open bathroom, open window. The word "NoModCons" flashes in my head with a red ballpoint star next to it. Though, looking around, I'm not sure if I see any conveniences, modern or otherwise.

I sure do know how to pick 'em. Over the phone, the landlord had said that I could look the place over before committing to the first month's rent. But given my savings, this was my only option.

Scanning the concrete floor painted a putrid sort of green, it's at least mildly reassuring that there isn't a masking tape outline of a body. At least if there had been one, they were courteous enough to remove the evidence before I got here.

…small favors, I guess.

The earthy smell of mold invades my nose, and I start to think about the abandoned factory I photographed years before. A fire had eaten a hole in the ceiling, and a decade or two of rain had poured in. This place was slightly better than that, and what did I expect for 45 bucks a month? Even if it's

Des Moines fucking Iowa.

I'm sure I could have found something cheaper out in the sticks, but living far away from everything without a car would have made the project impossible. The little money I have left should only go towards the essentials and the project itself. Anyway, I've seen much worse.

Bleach, that's step one. Step two, to be determined.

The apartment is roughly what I expected. A counter, a free-standing commode (no door or curtain) that looks like it's been there and never cleaned since the building was constructed sometime in the 1800s, but at least there's enough room to put my stuff. I open the bag containing all my worldly possessions: my Leica, Polaroid, a small mountain of film, a few markers and pens, the last six months of Art in America, a copy of *Grapefruit*, and three sets of clothes. Even at 150 square feet, there's more than enough space. So, at least I didn't get it in my head that this project needed to be on canvas.

I didn't expect the concrete floor, but it's nothing that a half-dozen blankets from a thrift store won't fix.

A pair of clogs walk past my window. I try to follow the legs up—but she disappears into the mystery of what's beyond my ceiling. I'll also have to buy something to cover that thing up. The idea of people being able to look down here at me whenever they want makes me feel more than a little anxious, and tension works its way up from the bottom of my belly until my fingers start to twitch, like a smoker who ran out when all the stores are closed.

I take out the Polaroid and set it on the counter. Reaching out, I press the shutter; the flash goes off. *First, you pull the front tab and then pull out the second to get the picture*, I recite to myself. I had picked up the brand new "Big Swinger" just before I left and read the instructions at least a dozen times on the ride here.

I lift the exposure paper and take a look at myself. My hand goes to my hair, or where it used to be. The hair is now in the garbage of some gas station restroom somewhere between there and here. One of many stops the bus took along the way. Next, the hand gingerly goes to my nose. As I look at the bandage across its bridge, it is nearly one huge pitch-black square splotch on the photograph.

It probably needs stitches. That isn't in the budget, either. It's just going to have to wait, or else I'll have to live with the scar. I peel off the bandage and take another picture. This time I can see the edges of the wound across my nose curling up into an Elvis sneer, pulled up to one side. Like a second mouth. I never asked for the first one. The asymmetry bothers me more than the gash itself. I look around the room for a mirror but come up empty.

In the picture, dust in the air catches the reflection of the flash, making white freckles like tiny snowflakes or flowers dapple across the tear in my skin. At least I don't look like me. That's the whole point of moving so far away, to be someone else. Right now, I'm the last person I'd want to be.

❦

Second day here, and I already have a job at a

diner. The owner said he didn't have anywhere else to put me than dishwashing until the bandage came off. *Wouldn't look right,* he said. *I don't need people thinking I'm beating up my employees any more than they already do.* And then he laughed so hard it sent him into a coughing fit, spit and sweat diffusing into the air like perfume at a cosmetic counter.

My hands jerked reflexively up to my chest. But I didn't say anything.

The less I have to talk to people, the better. I'm still working on my voice, and don't want to spoil any illusions.

I start work right away, and all they play all day is AM radio, saccharine and sweet. It's like the Carpenters and Osmonds started breeding together to take over the airwaves. Like the children from *Village of the Damned* but backed by the finest studio musicians the record labels have to offer. It could be worse. At least it's not a bunch of hippy shit.

I walk into the seating area after my shift. A man sitting at the end of the counter looks dried and crumbled into himself, his movements puppet-like and stiff.

Things grow down there, he says in a raspy feminine voice. His movements and speech are so slow that they'd be going backward if they could. *What?* I ask.

I feel an unwelcome hand on my shoulder, and I nearly collapse. *Don't mind him,* the owner offers. *He's always saying weird shit to people, especially people he's never seen before. It's just nonsense.* His voice hushes. *He comes here every day, and orders pancakes and coffee, sitting there pecking at his food and getting refills till we close.*

❀

The problem is that people spend more time talking than they do listening. I know. I'm guilty of it myself. The impulse to be heard is a potent drug. Most don't have the willpower to resist. And trying to understand anybody or anything outside of yourself is something the vast majority won't even begin to consider.

For example, my professors at Cranbrook have

been teaching the same way since before Jackson Pollock was a sperm. You would be hard-pressed to find a few who even thought photography was an art. Anything that didn't resemble a Rembrandt or a Renoir was entirely out of the question.

Something I forgot to ask about while taking the tour of the campus, I guess. I'll chalk it up to my naivete, as most of them hadn't kept up with art theory past the first World War. The idea that Dali, Rauschenberg, Warhol were their art, and what they produced was just secondary was something that most of them couldn't even wrap their head around, let alone actually teach and support in their students was just out of the question.

After a year of discussing my ideas with them, with a lot of gallery art buzzwords like "identity," "performance art," and "the lucid ephemeral," one of my teachers gave me a check for $200. For materials, getting away, he said. He claimed it was an artist grant he had applied for on my behalf. I didn't doubt that it came out of his pocket.

The next time I saw him, his hand found its way to my knee and started slowly moving up. I don't know if he took my silence as encouragement, but I couldn't have opened my mouth if I tried. Fortunately, someone came into the room, and I fled to the bus station a week early

※

I take out the Polaroid, set it on the counter. Reaching out, I press the shutter; the flash goes off. First, you pull the front tab and then pull out the second to get the picture. I lift the exposure paper and look at myself. The wound across the bridge of my nose is even bigger than in the last several shots, the edges spongy like old fruit. I figured, from looking at the stack of pictures, that it wasn't really dappled light or dust. It appears more like new skin starting to form, but that doesn't happen, does it? I should have paid more attention in biology.

Little splotches of white on the raw flesh underneath my skin.

I press the edges together, and rather than an Elvis snarl, I see a Cheshire grin. Alice has nothing on me, or rather that cat doesn't. In a book by Kenneth Anger, I remember reading that Disney would press his erect penis against little boys and girls when they would come and sit in "Uncle Walt's" lap. Maybe, that's when the last bit of my childhood illusions finally died, not that I had many to begin with.

After my father hit me, I never talked to him or my mother again. There was a handful of change sitting on the counter for me every Monday for lunch and other kid expenses. Never enough to last through Friday. We picked up our dinner plates and went to our respective areas every night. We were roommates. Nothing more.

The money disappeared when mom caught me waiting tables.

When I left for college, I didn't say goodbye.

※

My name is Gray Sorensen. I repeat to myself, a little higher, a little lower, and then back up a notch.

I'd spent the morning practicing a sob story about losing my ID, but the woman at the Ankeny DMV waved me off. Gray seemed as good as any name. She didn't ask any questions. Didn't even ask for proof. She said I should come back when I don't have the bandage anymore. It was *unsightly* and would be hard for people checking it to recognize me.

It's not like I need it for anything other than the project. I take the ID home and stick it in an envelope, already busting at the seams with Polaroids, along with my first month's rent notice.

MY name is Gray Sorensen.

My NAME is Gray Sorensen.

My name IS Gray Sorensen.

You can scrub your life of as many identifiers as you can, but people will always insist on a name.

Every piece of art needs one.

꽃

I wake up to the sound of my father breathing. I know it can't be him because he's dead, but his unmistakable presence lingers. I go over and turn on the single bulb dangling from the ceiling. There is nothing but the nest of blankets I stole from the donation pile outside a closed Salvation Army. I should feel bad about that, I think. I just don't.

Tears run down my face, but when I wipe them away, my hands are covered in white liquid tinged with a slight pinkness; must be pus from the wound. One month and 100 pictures later, it isn't looking any better. The rotten fruit pucker of its edges is deeply pockmarked. It even droops over the edge of my nose when I take the bandage off.

I take out the Polaroid, set it on the counter. Reaching out, I press the shutter; the flash goes off. First, you pull the front tab and then pull out the second to get the picture. I leave it in the envelope without looking at it.

Been feeling weak. Maybe the gash is making me anemic. Either way, I've been sleeping most of the hours I'm not at the diner. It's slowing down the project, but it should be better soon. I have months before I need to start curating the bits and pieces to see how I'll display this, what fragmented parts still need to be filled.

Narrowing down what ritzy galleries I should contact. What galleries represent Warhol? I'll have to check my list later. Might as well start at the top, at least the top of the places   I'd want "Gray" to be seen.

But when this comes out, is Gray just the subject or also the creator? Who am I when I start to try to parcel out who gets credit? Or is there a separation at all? After all this, will "Gray" become nothing, or do I?

🍥

Frankenstein stitches are the best I can do. The flesh sags around the crude, uneven loops of thread.

I picked up a small mirror, needle, and thread from Woolworths. I probably should have gotten something to disinfect it, or at least my face. At this point, I'm not sure it even matters. The smell of fresh soil seeps from my skin. Underneath it, the once raw red meat has nearly turned the color of boiled pork from the hundreds of little splotches knitting together.

HAIRS

❁

You've been hurt a long time. The old man says to me from the other side of the counter in his gravely androgynous voice. I reach to my face, but my hand ends up on my chest. *What do you mean?* I ask in a thin and wobbly voice that I've never heard come out of my mouth before.

Headlights go by the diner's windows and cast shadows of big fat snowflakes on the walls. A monochromatic light show that nobody asked for, but for a moment, I appreciate the distraction. A moment of reality in what has felt like a bad B-movie ever since I stepped off the bus in this town. A film that I have no conscious control of, though I wrote the script. Alone, in my dorm room, a lifetime ago.

❁

This basement is a meat locker. I feel sick. My body's sore in a way that's worse than any flu I've ever had. Did I come down with something? I see my breath as I cough. My chest feels heavy with congestion. Getting out of these blankets sounds like a hell, but it's time to take another photograph.

I lift the exposure paper and look at myself.

A small flower pokes out from between my uneven stitches, right on the bridge of my nose. A tiny white flower like they use as filler in bouquets. Half-stained pink from the ooze that continues to drip into my bandages every day.

I try to pluck it, but it makes me feel like I'm falling through a void.

I pull at the stitches, and they come out without any effort. Just the slow, uncomfortable feeling of floss being dragged across my gums. Tender and as deliberate as I can be until they're gone, and the skin falls loose again, now drooping down past my bottom lip.

I press the shutter; the flash goes off.

From the bottom of my vision, I see many of the flowers sprouting from the meat of my face. As if controlled by someone else, my hand goes to the loose skin and I tug. It rips like tissue paper. I keep going, and more flowers grow down my neck.

HAIRS

I press the shutter; the flash goes off. The previous photo falls to the floor, unexposed.

I keep pulling, and the skin is almost completely gone from my head and shoulders. It falls down my back like the hood of a jacket.

I press the shutter; the flash goes off. The previous one falls to the floor.

I pull at my collar, tugging like trying to rip off a shirt, and my skin comes away effortlessly. From the center of my chest, a single red flower springs up like a jack-in-the-box.

I grab the flower by the stem and once again feel faint as it comes loose.

Another picture falls to the floor.

IOWA

While producing Hairs, I originally left out several stories for different reasons. Two of these were published as the zine *Iowa*, the other two haven't seen the light of day until now.

If you don't like them, please pretend they're not here.

-Ira. Sept., 2024

Suicide Over Coffee

The exit to the fucking town was so overgrown with weeds and brush that if she hadn't been eyeing the side of the road like a priest on a playground, she probably would have missed it. Even so, she managed to do just that, only noticing the reflection of the sign in her rearview a dozen feet or so after passing it.

Three-point turns were nearly impossible on these small country roads, but she was able to manage.

The town was small, with the kind of rubbed-in dirt that no amount of urban flight money would be able to fix. This was the kind of town where she imagined that people kept stills. Iowa wasn't exactly known for its moonshine, but it was better than the thought that she was surrounded by labs full of jaw grinders.

Which was infinitely more likely in this neck

of the woods.

This was attested to by the teenage gas station clerk with janky homemade tattoos up both of her arms and neck. Who, when she smiled at Riley, flashed a quaint little grin that was more gaps than teeth.

Her debit card felt moist in her hand.

Thoughts of the few times that Riley had ended up scrubbing her bathroom until five in the morning snapped like a Polaroid flash in her head. Never smoke anything that someone hands you at a FaceCage show, her narrator scolded in the tone of an after school special. Point taken and remembered not too fondly.

The gas station looked like it was in a late stage of dry-rot and rust, spreading like an infection to everything that surrounded it—so much so she was half surprised when her car's engine turned over when she turned the keys. Well… her boss' car.

Well… it had been.

HAIRS

She had traded plates back in a small town outside of Ames, and now she was already halfway out of the state. Maybe, with any luck, nobody would notice yet another black Honda out of the thousands that dotted the road like deer who didn't get out of the way quickly enough.

She was careful not to steal a plate that was too recognizable. She always pictured the people who got their plates emblazoned with the name of a local sports mascot like "CYCRZY" were the types to come out on bended knee to polish their plates, giving them a little kiss before going back to their gated community from Sam's Club.

She looked in the back to make sure the briefcase that probably cost 2 or 3 months ' rent was still in the backseat. The case, that a couple of hours ago had also been her boss', sat there with a little gold plate. An engraved "T.C." gleamed in the afternoon sun.

Right now, she should have been wrist-deep in pointless paperwork that she wouldn't be able to make heads nor tails of. Instead, she watched as the heavy, bearded men wearing Pioneer Seed and John Deere hats walked out of the station with fistfuls of scratch-offs. Somehow, still managing to wrangle wads of chew into their lip. One after another. It was almost like they were clones.

A conspiracy danced around in her head for a few seconds, before she remembered that most small Iowa towns around here were populated with men who looked exactly like this. Related to each other to the point of inbreeding, maybe, but who would be mass producing this variety of specimen?

A sense of urgency pressed hard into her throat. Not because of these rednecks, but rather because she remembered that this was supposed to her escape. This was her one chance to get out of Iowa, and she wasn't going to screw it up by gawking at a bunch of Jethros.

A shock of adrenaline hit her heart as she put the car into gear, and she tried to inconspicuously tear out of the parking lot as fast as possible. She had already seen a green truck with bronze testicles hanging from the back bumper do it. She didn't think that anybody would notice her doing the same.

The roads in town didn't look like they had been replaced since Kennedy was in office. The car was newer, and the shocks were good, but it still made for a jarring ride as she drove past the unevenly spaced houses on the way out of town.

Within minutes, she was back out into the farms. Shortly after, the car started shaking violently.
What the fuck? She yelled at nobody.

Getting out of the car, she saw that one of her tires was cartoonishly blown.

Waving down a conspicuously out of place Prius as it passed, she flipped it off when it didn't stop.
Minutes passed, and the road was deserted with the kind of stillness that made her feel like any minute the boogeyman would jump out.

It, fortunately, didn't.

With the weight of the briefcase in her hand,

it felt like Riley had been walking for hours, but it couldn't have been more than 20 minutes. With her adrenaline high, it felt like more like two. She asked herself over and over what she had gotten herself into, like a mantra of regret that wouldn't just let her be.

Every sideroad looked the same, dust and gravel and no house in sight. The sun felt like it had specifically selected her to beat down on today. Like she was under god's magnifying glass, an ant that had just begun to sizzle.

The humid air dragged her further down with every step, and the smell of shit stung her nose. "Well, I guess this means I'm still in Iowa," she mumbled to herself as she continued. The fantasy of being anywhere but here still played repeatedly in her mind, like one of those early movies that were just loops of the same pictures into forever.

It didn't matter where the new place was, or what she would do once she got there, but it was the fact that it wouldn't be the same that held all the magic in the world for her. She had barely been out of the state for much of her 23 years. Let alone, anywhere she felt like let her escape from the "Iowa nice" Midwest faces that haunted her even in her dreams.

In the city, or even in these small towns, there was the oppression of being put upon by the repression of others that always seemed to say "everything's going to be okay," even when they were the furthest thing from that. For the thousandth time since starting this little walk, she realized it was pretty far from o-fucking-k.

She had looked out at the endless stream of identical days before her and knew that she had to risk everything in order to avoid it. Even if these new days were just a different flavor of drudgery, at least they would be somewhere else under the indifferent sky. She realized that she had turned away from existence and the life in front of her at every opportunity. Choosing to work 10 hours a day for minimum wage at a coffee shop that nobody visited, except for the owner's "friends," who didn't pay, or even tip.

After all, Jesus hadn't wept for the passing of his friend, she mused, or even that he himself would soon meet the same fate. He wept because it truly didn't matter.

She started to daydream about how far the contents of the briefcase would get her. The east coast? The west coast? Somewhere out of America? She wasn't entirely sure how much was in there; she just knew it had to be more than she had ever had at any one time in her life. It wasn't the first time that she had been asked to deliver one of these briefcases, but the conspicuous questionability of both the boss that handed it to her and the man that she would meet always made her feel like the contents had to be more valuable than she was to them.

Not that a middle management barista in a flailing coffee shop was much value to anybody. Yet they kept the place open, why? It had to have something to do with what was in this briefcase. She envisioned stacks and stacks of money or, at the very least, enough drugs to buy her a new life.

Or from the look of the owner's "friends," maybe she was looking to get killed. Maybe, just maybe, this is her convoluted way of choosing suicide over coffee.

Treehouse

Driving on gravel roads, alone at night in the middle of Iowa, was something I did because I didn't have enough money to develop a healthy drug or alcohol problem. Well, at least, when I was right out of high school. How I was able to pull together the money for gas and cigarettes consistently is something that is now beyond me.

God knows that there wasn't any place to work out in the middle of the cornfields.

One night, I found myself turning at random down one of these unlit roads, when from out of nowhere, a DEAD END sign jumped up in front of my car. The momentum of my sudden stop propelled me into the steering wheel. If I had been wearing my seat belt, my head would probably have not come within inches of the lit cigarette in my hand.

HAIRS

The orange ring that glowed faintly under the ash still glowed after I closed my eyes.

I could hear the hail of rocks hit the sign over the sound of Surfer Rosa playing from the cassette deck. My cigarette burned with annoyance. Biting into the filter, I started cranking the wheel of my red Geo Metro, whose power steering had died long before I had been given the keys by my older brother.

I ejected the tape and threw it on the passenger seat. A fashionable friend had copied it for me. My unpopular friend had died with the cassette in his car. I always felt a little weird having it in mine. It went on, to show me, for playing it so loud to defy the curse that had been laid upon it.

The moon looked down apathetically. I felt like giving it the finger, but ash fell into my lap, so instead I tried to swat it away with my one free hand.

One degree at a time, I began my 300-point turn. Kicking up so much dust and rock that I could hardly breathe, let alone see what was going on outside my front window. A window that had already been spiderwebbed by some other incident that had already been forgotten in the endless days of nothing to do.

I flicked the cigarette out and watched it launch a dozen fireflies into the air before they blinked out of existence, as if they had never lived at all. I felt something for their brief lives, but I couldn't for the life of me think of what that could be.

My arms started to hurt, partly from the sudden impact, partly because I had been cranking the steering wheel with every fiber of my being just to get it to move yet another half inch each time I backed up and started again.

Fuck.

On my hundredth attempt trying to turn the meek machine around, I could feel that the car wasn't going forward anymore. I pulled the gear shift into reverse. The car wasn't going that way either. The sudden urge to put it into neutral and try to push it crossed my mind, but the thought of it rolling farther into one of the ditches on the sides of the road put an end to that pretty quick.

Anyway, it was just fuck-o me here. God only knows what would happen if I were to try to do something heroic on my own. I'd probably find a way to run myself over. At least, that's what I had thought at the time. I had heard too many stories of people getting flattened by their own cars trying to get them out of the snow in January. Seemed like a shitty way to go.

Putting on the emergency brake, I abandoned ship.

People romanticize the silence that you're supposed to be able to appreciate in the middle of nowhere, but that night was loud as hell. Every member of the animal kingdom was out there making noise, at least the ones that weren't trying to eat me alive.

You never hear the sound of the mosquitoes that are trying to feed on you. Just like the bullets that you don't manage to dodge.

It had to have been at least a mile to the first house. All the lights were out, but there were plenty of trucks there. A couple of knocks produced nothing. Hell, if I lived out in the middle of godknowswhere and someone knocked on my door past midnight, I'm sure I wouldn't have answered the door for me either.

I could have been a serial killer, for all they knew.

I pictured the American Gothic couple lying in bed with pistols, waiting for the long-haired druggie freak to pass them by. It was the Clinton administration, but some of these people out here still looked and acted like it was the early '60s.

The world is always changing, rarely for the better. Though there are these pockets, especially out here on the perimeter that don't get touched. There's something beautiful about that, but it still meant that I had to walk my ass back home — not knowing which way that was.

HAIRS

The night was... something. Hot, I guess. Stifling and precisely the same as too many others would be closer to the mark. Small gray stones that shone brightly in the moonlight kept stabbing my feet when I pulled them out of my shoes.

Well, I guess I was putting in my exercise for the year, I thought to myself. I hadn't walked this far since the time my friend whose car I had fished Surfer Rosa out of had pulled a similar fuck-up with his car in the middle of a dirt road that ran through a small woods. The 5 of us had to walk back to town.

We thought it had been funny enough to make a movie out of. It wasn't.

We all tried to figure out who would play us in the movie. I was nominated Kevin Smith. I remember thinking that I should start working out after that. I didn't. This walk was my first real exercise in the year since.

How he could have ended up playing a high schooler was improbable, anyway. Fuck that, I thought. I would have been proud to have been portrayed by Silent Bob. I scratched the bug bites that I could feel rising up just underneath my shirt on my ample stomach.

When I saw the white Christmas lights on the trees in a small area up ahead, I thought that it must have been a weird joke, but then I started to remember the school-wide legend of the guy who had lost his wife and had built a house in a tree out in the middle of nowhere. There was barbed wire fence all around the patch of land.

I could see the lights glaring from inside the house that looked like something an upscale Ewok would live in.

I stopped and stared at this monument to a memory that someone had built just to escape after they couldn't handle reality anymore, and I envied that. I knew that I had no way of making my own escape.

When and if I ever got home, I would just go to sleep in my tiny room in my parents' house, and then wake up the next day and have to figure my way out of the nothing that my life had so far amounted to.

The world was my oyster, rotten and closed at the bottom of the bucket.

Cherry Mango

The one-act play Mango Cherry appeared in my book Endless Now.

> "There have been times in the past when people thought the end of the world was coming, and so forth, but never anything like this."
>
> — Ronald "Bedtime for Bonzo" Reagan

"I had a dream about you last night," Nick timidly shouted over the dull and repetitive party music that bled into the claustrophobically small bathroom, mainly consisting of Thud, Thud, Thud, and odd siren noises.

"Ugh… don't tell me about it. I hate hearing about people's dreams. Even… err… especially… if they're about me," Warren shouted over his shoulder towards Nick, who sat on the toilet while making sure that he was looking flawless in the bathroom mirror.

"It's just too telling," he continued. "I have no desire to have a look into other people's psyches. It's unnerving, like sending me an unsolicited link to your OnlyFans account."

"It's nothing like…"

"Says you, I'm too much of an egomaniacal armchair psychologist not to read into it. It's uncomfortable." Warren removes a toothbrush from the host's cabinet and starts dry brushing his teeth. "So, sorry… but this is a hard pass from me."

"… ok."

"Don't turn all passive-aggressive on me. Would you prefer me standing here silently resenting you as you're doing a striptease of your thoughts in front of me?"

"I said, it's not…"

"… like that, I know. I'd have even more

questions about your sanity, or your lack thereof, if you were having sex dreams about me. However, sharing your dreams is far too close for comfort, and I don't feel comfortable being that intimate with anyone, let alone you. No offense."

"Are you that shallow that you think that just because you were in it, it has anything to do with you?"

"Again, I know that it has nothing to do with me, other than it had everything to do with me. It's just the way that it makes me feel." Warren gave him a faux-pity look through the mirror. "If you were to whip out your prick and start waving it around suddenly, it would make me feel the same way. Uncomfortable and slightly embarrassed for you."

Nick and Warren sat there for a minute, until the door started thudding with a police knock. They stared at each other with the gravity of civilians, waiting for a WWII bomber to pass overhead.

"Quit sucking each other off in there!" an

annoyed voice bellowed from the other side of the door.

"We've only got copula lines left. Give us a sec!" Warren yelled back, shaking his head no to Nick, whom he could read and was wondering if he was holding.

There was a big enough silence from the other side of the door to leave room for Jesus. "Can…"

"No!" Nick and Warren yelled back in unison, very loud but clearly not angry.

Another third-trimester pause, both waiting for a response that never comes. After several seconds, they both relax. "Was that Frankie?" Nick asked, knowing full well that it was.

"Sounded like him."

"I thought he was…"

"From what I heard, they let him go." Warren's eyes rolled so far back into his head that you could hear his optic nerves creaking like wet leather. "The police said the video was from the internet, so they couldn't prove that she was under eighteen."

"Well, that's comforting. We need to get Chris Maloney on that shit!"

Warren makes the Law and Order "Ba Bom!" sound. "There are companies online that make perfectly legal movies for freaks like him. Have you seen his girlfriend? He has a type. Unfortunately, that type is girls who look like Rugrats."

"Sick shit."

"The sickest," Warren retorts while using the host's toothbrush on his eyebrows. "Speaking of sick," he says and points to a spot on his neck with the brush. "Does this look like a goiter?"

"What?"

Warren starts waving the brush dismissively. "Nothing, never mind, I forgot you were a Russian lit major."

"Ooook."

"I've got to take a leak." Nick gets off the toilet and passes Warren. However, the space is too small for this to happen with grace or elegance. First, they try to pass each other crotch-to-crotch, then ass-to-ass, and finally settle on the crotch to ass. Nick turns to face the door as Warren starts to piss.

"Beckett!" Warren yells.

"What?"

"I was quoting—or rather, misquoting Godot. Because we're here waiting."

Nick gives the back of Warren's head an exaggerated "Ohhhh…" face.

"Something about 'looks like a goiter.' I don't know. The line always stuck out to me, because you don't hear 'goiter' conversationally."

"We're waiting for something?"

"I don't know if we're waiting for something." Warren flushes and zips up. "But we're not doing anything, either." Nick and Warren do their little dance again, and Warren starts primping once more, not having washed his hands.

"Do you believe in aliens?" Nick asked, with the innocence of a toddler, questioning the color of the sky.

"What? I mean statistically."

"No, I mean right here, right now, on this planet, this city, this block, maybe even this house."

Warren arched his eyebrow. "Uhhh… are you a closet Q or something?"

"No, it's just that dream…" Warren stares Nick down with a not this shit again look. "It was this exact situation. Same conversation, same everything."

"Ohhhhhkay?"

Outside the room, the music's thud, thud, thud suddenly stops, and a new song doesn't kick in.

"Is the party over?" Nick whispers in the same lost child manner as before.

"I don't know. Sounds that way? Though I don't hear anyone leaving... Cops?" Warren's whisper matches Nick's.

"In this neighborhood?"

"Yeah... They seem like the kind of people who would have made sure nobody around here would have called in a complaint."

The two of them stare at each other a few moments longer than either of them is comfortable, looking mildly distressed.

"Do you think the world has ended?" Nick asks, wide-eyed and innocent.

"Don't be ridiculous," Warren answered, too

quick to be convincing.

"Then you open the door."

They both stare at the doorknob, trying to Jedi mind trick it open, but then the music starts.

"Alllll… right. Should we make an appearance now?"

"Maybe later," Nick answers, as he turns away from the door and starts staring again at the back of Warren's head.

SOFT

> "I think I'm in hell, therefore I am."
>
> —Arthur Rimbaud

I am a fifth-generation bootleg of myself. A recording of a recording of a recording of a… All background noise and soft edges, a drone with no beginning or end, a constant now of a mildly occupied frequency. I exist to separate the nothingness from the somethingness, no matter how insignificant my disruption to non-existence might be.

My dreams were to perform in gleaming white, surgically white rooms, all 90-degree angles, and the kind of bland lighting that only someone who never once had to worry about pulling a day job while going to school would be able to design. The kind of rooms that would make Marina Abramovic's granny panties moist.

Middle-class aspiration of decadence collapses under the weight of old money. Once you finally get there, it's no longer Versace and Versailles. It's $250 plain gray polos that look the same as a $10 Walmart special.

I can't remember the last time I saw a perfect angle. Tonight, it's a country club on the outskirts of Cedar Rapids. Cigarette smoke fills the air, wood panels cover the walls, and my bare feet tread through shag carpeting that feels like it hasn't been vacuumed since it was installed somewhere in the mid-last century.

Hell isn't other people. Hell is doing the thing that you love night after night to uncaring, indifferent audiences in the performance art equivalent of the chitlin circuit. If you were to tell Yoko Ono or (not that) Nick Cave that places like this exist, they would scoff in incredulity. I wouldn't have known either, if I didn't need to eat.

My jaw hurts from chewing. The world is the taste of dirty pennies. It's all I can taste... hear...

smell. I feel the blood running down the back of my throat. However, observations seep into me like osmosis. I'm not consciously aware of anything, but my senses are heightened. Somehow, I'm as omnipotent as Santa Claus.

When I asked them to play some Kali Malone, they looked at me blankly, same when I asked for anything neo-classical. So I asked for something soft, to create "a mood." My skin bristles as this-decade country music crawls through the not-so-discreetly recessed speakers and into my ears.

A '70s snuff film plays behind me, over me, around me. I can tell it's the '70s by the size of the bush on the girl being vivisectioned. I would complain that it was distracting from the show, but at these types of venues, I've learned to just do the work. Its flickering light crisscrosses my body, illuminating the veneer-perfect topographical moon maps of my scars. It would be oh so beautiful if it weren't such a goddamn waste.

Would you die for modern art? At least

conceptually? There are a big B—billion mini-Hirsts who are willing to kill, stick pins through things, and display, but nobody is willing to sacrifice anything, let alone themselves. They aren't willing to give anything of themselves to their audience. This is my body, Pastor Keith's voice crawls from the back of my brain a childhood memory, made not too many miles away from here.

A billboard-sized R. Crumb fills my brain. "I'm dying up here," the crucified man yells at the yuppies mingling. I should be so lucky. I mock myself. Fuck, I wish I could draw like Crumb. I could never draw anything representational. Instead, I got drawn to theory classes. The distance between craftspeople/illustrators and true artists is miles, but I still can't help wonder how my life would be different, if pencils didn't lie in my hand like dead fish.

I am art.

The host laughs in the back, all missing teeth and escaping cigar smoke. His money was green, and he had the space. So, this is where my judgement ends. I've been doing this far too long, for far too many people to really pass judgement on anyone. Well, that's not true, I do, but I admit that I'm a hypocrite.

A row of hillbillies playing nouveau riche watch my every move. Pricks in hand, the sound of their cocks slithering through their wrinkled fingers, and their wheezing is almost enough to put me off my meal.

I had been popular for a moment in the world of real money, but like everything else, these things come and go in phases. Right now, auto-cannibalism is so pre-COVID. I chew and chew and chew, it's worse than any steak at even the cheapest steakhouses you can think of. My blood pools around my left arm, the bite looking Apple logo perfect.

Jesus wept; it was that goddamn beautiful.